COLOUR
BANJO

COCO BANJO

AND THE SUPER WOW SURPRISE

N. J. GEMMELL

RANDOM HOUSE AUSTRALIA

A Random House book
Published by Random House Australia Pty Ltd
Level 3, 100 Pacific Highway, North Sydney NSW 2060
www.randomhouse.com.au

Penguin
Random House
Australia

First published by Random House Australia in 2016

Random House Books is part of the Penguin Random House group of companies
whose addresses can be found at global.penguinrandomhouse.com.

National Library of Australia
Cataloguing-in-Publication Entry

Creator: Gemmell, N.J., author, illustrator
Title: Coco Banjo and the super wow surprise / N.J. Gemmell
ISBN: 978 0 85798 737 2 (paperback)
Series: Gemmell, N.J. Coco Banjo; 3
Target Audience: For primary school age
Subjects: Surprise – Juvenile fiction. Holidays – Juvenile fiction. Children's
stories.
Dewey Number: A823.3

Cover and internal illustration by N.J. Gemmell
Cover and internal design and typesetting by Astred Hicks, designcherry
Printed in Australia by Griffin Press, an accredited ISO AS/NZS 14001:2004
Environmental Management System printer

Random House Australia uses papers that are natural, renewable and recyclable
products and made from wood grown in sustainable forests. The logging
and manufacturing processes are expected to conform to the environmental
regulations of the country of origin.

To my amazing mum
– a Clem in spirit.

It was the very first morning of the summer holidays.

yiPPeeeeee!

Coco Banjo put on her brand new, tiger-striped wetsuit.

Oh, all right, it was a bit hot for it because it was December in Sydney. But excuse me, our girl hero **LOVED IT ANYWAY.**

It's her new favourite thing.

COCO whooshed down the silver mega-slide in the middle of her secret home on Sydney Harbour (the one and only **CHA CHA ISLAND**). She landed on a pile of enormous red, pink and orange velvet cushions in the cinema pod.

It was **9 a.m.!**

Time for Coco's mum, **Clem**, to appear on the screen!

And she was going to be **home** in living, breathing real life very **SOOOOOON!**

Quick, Coco, international fashion stylists never have long.

Clem was in New York at the moment. She was styling **Queen Blah Blah** (the latest girl-rapper sensation) for her debut concert at Madison Square Garden.

Coco pressed the button to connect to her mum. She heard a voice through the speaker.

Fabulous, darling, now go forth and seize this glorious day.

Clem wants everyone to seize every day. Gloriously.

Hang on. **COCO** was confused. **Who** was Clem talking to? Her, or Queen Blah Blah?

Mum could get very distracted by her **super-busy** job and, er, sometimes it was hard to tell what was going on.

She's talking to you, darling, you.

And she'll be home soon, remember.

'Is that my **number 1** Missy Princess Pie?' laughed Clem to Coco.

'Mrs Mumpy Pie!' Coco squealed.

'Big tick for that outfit, girl.'

'It matches my tiger-striped rowboat. And onesie. And pillows. And toothbrush.'

Coco high-fived the screen. **Clem** high-fived back.

'Now run outside, darling,' Clem said. 'There's a surprise for you. On a boat.'

(Clem was good at *mad* and *glorious* surprises. Because she wasn't home very often.)

What is it? What?

Coco was so **excited** she didn't stop to say goodbye to Clem. She:

☑ **Leapt** onto the golden fireman's rope that dangled through the centre of the house

☑ **Climbed** up, up, up to the light

☑ **Burst** outside into a dazzling Sydney morning

☑ **Waved** at **Wing** and **Wang**, her bestest penguin friends, who wiggled and jiggled in greeting.

tall blue sky

Wang

Wing

sparkling harbour

Oh happy day!

DAISY the dolphin, Coco's best-ever dolphin friend, flapped her little flipper right near the shore.

Coco blew Daisy a *KISS* and tossed her a *fish* from the retro beachside mini-[fridge]

Expertly caught

Happiest of endlessly summery happy days!

Coco stood on her tippy-toes and squinted through a long, brass telescope on its stand. **CLEM** had bought it in London. It came from one of the earliest **convict** ships that sailed to Sydney.

Coco swivelled it to look around the harbour. What on earth was her mum talking about?

Bingo. The most fabulous sight:

Coco's bestest friend, Narianna Nicketson (known as **N**). Heading straight for her. In N's brand new, adorable red-spotted rowboat that she got for her birthday.

Partners in crime.

Especially during summer holidays.

At the front of 's boat was an extremely **mysterious** object.

A **HUGE** box. Covered, most thrillingly, in tiger–striped fabric. And wrapped in an enormous black *feather* boa tied in a bow at the top.

Very Clem

What's going on?

It was the most **exciting**, deliciously **unknowable** object Coco had ever seen.

And she had no idea why it was arriving except for Clem's **one** little clue.

Do you know?

Captain  reached little
Cha-Cha-licious beach.

'Ship ahoy!' she yelled.

Her waving arms then crisply indicated:

SECRET SIGNAL Number

MEANING ▷ We've got all day to play here,

girlfriend. Mrs N won't start

getting hysterical until teatime.

Just what the doctor ordered for summer holidays.

The two girls **dragged** the rowboat up the sand above the high tide mark.

Then they stared at the mysterious object in front of them, with its enticing bow.

'Your mum was in cahoots with my mum about it,'  said. 'But my mum wouldn't tell me anything. Meanie.'

N giggled. 'My strict instructions were to just deliver it and . . .'

'What? What?' COCO felt as though she was going to burst.

'Play. With it. ALL DAY.'

Huh?

Just then the tiger-striped object **jUmPed**.

The girls leapt back.

The box **shook**.

Rattled.

And **yelped.**

Yelped?

Yes.
Yelped.

Coco and looked at each other and rushed forward. Could it be? Could it?

They **whipped** off the feather boa.
Tore open the tiger–striped wrapping.

Inside, waiting for them, was the **tiniest**, *fluffiest* bundle of puppy–licious puppyness they had ever seen.

No little dog had ever been **cuter** in the history of **cuteness**.

Swoon, Swoon, Swoon.

16

There was only one thing for the two besties to do:

Again. And again. And again.

Brand new puppies tend to have this effect.

Coco gently lifted the bundle of adorable-ness from the cage. Her tickles and cuddles were rewarded by little snuffles and licky kisses.

Coco's fingers found a clasp on the barrel  under the puppy's neck. She sprang it open. Inside was a tiny roll of paper.

A secret note!

Missy Princess Pie,

I'll be home eventually. Eeeek. Double eeek. I promise. I just, er, can't say when. Sorry. Double sorry. Work is so, so, so busy right now.

But in the meantime... a puppy!

Just for you!

I know you've wanted one for, like, ever. And I know you'll be a hugely responsible big sister to it. All those endless promises to feed a puppy, train it and love it to bits. Go for it, my darling. HAVE FUN!

♥ove M.M.P.*

*Mrs Mumpy Pie ♥♥♥

Well, that's one spectacular way of saying you're not coming back soon.

19

A tight, prickly, glittery ball of **sadness** was swelling deep in Coco's heart. Tears were jostling in her eyes,  wanting to spill out. Wanting to spoil this most delicious of summer holiday days.

Because **Clem** was not coming home any time soon. As usual.

Clem is always doing this.

Coco snuggled her brand new little friend close. She should have been the happiest girl in the world right now.

Sigh. **But** she wasn't.

'What will you call him?' asked softly, tickling the puppy around its ears.

'*Ludo*,' **COCO** said softly.

Because:

(a) she had always **loved** that name, and

(b) it meant *playful*, *cheeky* and **happy** (from the word 'ludic').

Which is what Coco usually, always, absolutely was.

Great name, Coco.

But at that moment, she felt anything but
happy.

You know, **Coco's** life might look amazing. Dazzling. Incredible. A puppy–licious riot of pop–tastic–ness.

But it's not. In fact, there are a **lot** of things you might have that she doesn't:

Coco felt the difference. **Hugely.** But what she had learnt was that it was no good having a big, grumpy, turtle face and bringing everyone down around you – no matter how sad you felt.

As *Clem* said: you have to be a heart-lifter in life. Not a heart-sinker.

You have to make people feel good about themselves. Because that will make you feel good about yourself.

So . . . *Onward* and

UPWARD. *Atta girl.*

'Hey, gang, let's go shopping!' Coco whooped with glee. 'Someone around here needs some puppy food.'

I'm hungry.

N, cheered. *Ludo* gave a happy yelp.

They found a wicker basket with a handle and a velvet cushion for Ludo. He showed his thanks by widdling on the cushion.

Hmmmm.

Cheeky Ludo. The girls wondered if there was such a thing as puppy nappies.

Wait until he starts **pooing** on the cushion.

Where's a puppy school when you need one?

They had a LOT to learn about dogs.

The girls rowed across to Cadi Beach, **COCO** in her tiger-striped boat , **N** in her spotty one.

Everyone seemed to be at the Banksia Bay supermarket.

In Aisle **1**:

Jay Page. Trying to take the broccoli and brussels sprouts that his father was putting in the trolley back out again.

I've got a great name for your new pet, Coco.

PUP-U-LAR. How about that?

Er, no thanks, Jay.

27

In Aisle  :

Their teacher, **Miss Bonkiss**. She shrieked when she saw the girls. 'Students! I'm allergic to students on holidays! I break out in a **rash** if I see one!'

Her horrified face then cracked into a **grin**. She rushed forward and gave N and Coco a big **cuddle**.

Dashing around the corner from Aisle **3**, to check out all the commotion:

Mr Patilla (Gorilla). Looking very . . . **hairy**.

Dusti, Dusti, are you okay?

Latest cycling gear for gents

quinoa

kale

protein powder

COCO and **N** looked at each other. Miss Bonkiss and Mr Patilla? Two **teachers?** Together?

Coco and N ran away, *giggling*.

What would the mummies of Banksia Bay Public think of this news?

In Aisle , Coco and N ran slap–bang into:

Miss Trample. In her holiday **finest**.

*A **very** Miss Trample basket*

Her shopping basket was **FULL** of 6 boxes

of oats, 8 packets of prunes and

Gee, that'll be a fun house over the holidays.

10 rolls of toilet paper.

Coco and '**N**' were speechless.

Unheard of in Coco-land.

Miss Trample glared at the little basket Coco was carrying. At a startled **Ludo** staring straight back at her.

'Dogs are **not** allowed in supermarkets, Coco Banjo,' Miss Trample said. 'And of course it would be **you** who flouts that rule, wouldn't it? Where's your **mother** to keep you in check? Hmm?'

Coco bit her lip. Felt about a centimetre tall. Miss Trample was good at making her feel this small.

But no one else said Ludo wasn't allowed here.

'Your mother isn't with you these holidays, is she?' The headmistress smiled in triumph, as though she had known all along. 'She's never, ever with you, is she, Coco Banjo?'

Then Miss Trample leaned right in close. Curled her lip. Shivered in disgust.

'And it shows.'

 Coco would **not** cry, would **not** cry.

But hey, sometimes it's hard not to.

pushed in between Miss Trample and her bestest best friend. She was having **none** of it.

Excuse me. Coco Banjo is the most amazing girl I've ever met. The kindest. Funniest. Bravest. She never complains. Never cries. Even when she scrapes her knee in the playground, and even when you make her do her 9 times tables 200 times and ban her from the school disco. Miss Trample, you WANT her to cry, don't you! Coco's the only one you've never cracked. But she's TOO STRONG. Plus, she's not scared of the dark. She's not scared of being by herself. She has more BRAVENESS than most people have in their little pinkie and I can say that to you because we're on SUMMER HOLIDAYS and you're NOT our BOSS **ANYMORE.**

Wow, N. That was **magnificent.**

33

 stopped. She went bright red. Because she had remembered something rather crucial . . .

Ooops.

N had remembered that she was the GOODEST GOOD GIRL of BANKSIA BAY PUBLIC.

And that Miss Trample would be her **boss** all over again, in 6 weeks. And Miss Trample had a very long memory.

Who cares? onya, N!

Later that day, the light was softening and sinking in the west. Everything  with the force of the sun.

 and  had spent the day:

 Grocery shopping

 Painting toenails and fingernails

 Braiding hair

 Dancing with *Wing and Wang*

 Adoring *Ludo*

Summer holidays get filled up really quickly.

 Creating a film trailer involving a lost island

 Stand-up paddle boarding (and, er, falling off)

Practising their synchronised swimming routine

Composing a brand new song for their **'En-Cee'** ← get it? superstar, two-person singing act.

One sunny day, I walked away...

Ooooo Ooooh!

Their aim: World domination. No less.

37

went home and *Coco* was now all alone. The last of the sun slipped behind the hills and the air was suddenly **cold**.

Coco was fishing off her favourite boulder,

Jump Rock.

Which N is not allowed to jump off.

Coco never ate the *fish* she caught, but *DAISY* appreciated them. And *Ludo* was having fun leaping up for them as Coco flung them into the water.

Ludo's big on playing - just like Coco.

To stop **Big, Horrible, Yukky Thoughts** crowding in – like Clem not coming home anytime soon – Coco tried to think of as many different kinds of marine life that live in Sydney Harbour  as she could.

She knew there were almost **600** different species. But today she could only think of **20.**

Can you beat Coco? Turn the page for the ones she can remember.

stargazers silky sharks

freshwater
eels

Painted
stinkfish

unicorn
Leather
jacket
fish

Porcupinefishes

Velvet fishes

Blind
sharks
flying fishes

Manta rays

And did we mention
the semi-aquatic species
called Sea-Crazy Little
Mer-girls?

Also known as
Coco and N.

41

Suddenly, from behind Jump Rock, there was a loud **pinging** noise.

It was the **Clanging Clem Conversation ALERTER** springing into action.

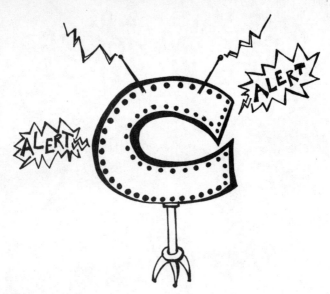

Clem was on the line!

Quick, Coco. Your mum's never around for long!

Coco scooped up *Ludo*, dashed inside and whooshed down the mega–slide, with the puppy held carefully in her arms the whole way. **WOW**

'**THANK YOU** for my present, Clem,' said Coco.

She held up Ludo for Clem to admire. Then she bit her lip and buried her face in Ludo's **softness**.

'**CLEM** turned her head to one side. 'Oooooh, he's adorable. But, Coco, what's wrong?'

Coco can't bear to say it.

'Missy Princess Pie,' Clem continued, 'you can tell me **anything**, you know that. Because I'm your mother. And I might just understand. **Try** me.'

Coco took a **deep** breath. Tried to stop the **wobble** in her voice. Then said, 'You said you'll be home "eventually". Which means forever. I just want you here so we can do **Tick Tock** ...'

'Oh,' Clem said. There was a thick, prickly **silence**

Tick tock, tick tock, it's **Clem** on the dot on the cuddle-time clock.

Oh dear.

Then it was as though a light bulb  went on in °ᏩᏝᏋᎷᏚₑ head. She smiled her most dazzling smile – which is exactly the same as her daughter's.

There's something I've been saving for a long time, waiting for the right moment. Now it's time. It's so exciting. It's time for ... the SKIP BACK MACHINE!!!

The ... what, Clem?

Clem started barking out instructions left, right and centre.

'A secret door!'

'Behind my Japanese kimono collection.'

'A **huge** machine!'

'I add to it whenever I'm back!'

'Wheel it out!'

'Set it up in **front** of my bed!'

'Pedal the pedals to get it **started**!'

'Then lie on the bed and let the glories of the **Skip Back Machine** wash over you!'

Clem winked. ⊙ ✺ 'Then, when you've had your fill of it – which will be never, ever, ever – get me back on the screen. Because I have some **more** exciting news for you, girly girl . . .'

Run Coco, run!

46

 raced to **Clem's** room. She:

- **Threw** open the cupboard

- **Waded** through the silk kimonos

- **Located** the secret door she'd never noticed.

And behind it she found . . .

48

Coco dragged the Skip Back Machine out and pushed it into the middle of **Clem's** bedroom.

The machine had two **pedals**, like a bicycle. Coco climbed onto its red velvet seat and started pedalling.

Faster, faster, faster...

The Skip Back Machine **whirred**, **burped**, **jolted** and then *hummed*.

Fairy lights sprang on, all over it. Oh! Little puffs of smoke shot out. Oh! Would it bring back Clem super-fast?

Then a voice from **deep** inside it declared . . .

It talks too?

49

'Sit back, relax, and make yourself comfortable, Miss Coco Banjo. The ride of your life is about to begin.'

It was Clem's voice doing the talking, and it was instantly soothing.

Coco jumped off the pedals and leaned back on Clem's 24 pillows on her super-wide bed. Put her arms behind her head.

That Clem is one clever lady.

 the voice said.

 most certainly did.

The Skip Back Machine threw thousands of twinkling lights onto the ceiling, the walls, the floor.

They **Spun**. **Danced**. Changed **colour**.

Oooh!

Then the room softly filled with a familiar lullaby.

It was an old lullaby that,  used to sing to COCO, endlessly, when she was tiny.

Feeling sleeeeeepy...

The song stopped. The *soothing* voice continued.

 rolled into a sleeping position with her hands together, under her cheek, as she listened.

"Once Upon a time...

Oh splendid! We do **love** a story.

'A mummy far, far away, in Sydney, Australia, received the greatest gift she could ever be given. A little baby. But not just any little baby. Oh no...'

On the wall Coco's name flashed up in movie-star lights. Then the Skip Back Machine started playing home videos and photos of wonderful moments of her growing up, with her mum.

There were all their favourite songs and films, and snippets of books they had read together, and nursery rhymes, and poems.

Awwww.

54

Clem's Skip Back Machine was skipping back through **Coco's** entire life, and all the **Joy** she had given Clem.

Next were all the pictures and cards and books that Coco had made for Clem over the years. Ever since Coco could hold a pencil and draw. Even if it was just a scribble.

Clem had kept every single **one!**

They meant **that** much to her!

Double awwwww.

Then, in a starburst of dazzling light, the Skip Back Machine played all the little snippets of wisdom that Clem had said to Coco over the years:

The screen faded slowly to an old picture of **Clem** cuddling **Coco** in their matching tiger–striped onesies.

Tick tock tick tock, it's Clem on the dot on the cuddle-time clock.

There was one last voice-over:

I hope you've enjoyed your skip Back experience, Captain Banjo the Courageous of Cha Cha Island. Remember, I'm always here for you when you need me. And I'll be home soon. I promise!'

What a machine.

Coco blew the screen a kiss. *Ludo* licked her cheek. She felt all glittery and happy–sad, filled up with memories and loneliness and giggles and love.

She lay on her back on the bed with her two feet in the air. Ludo was perched on her bare soles way up high.

Then Coco **remembered** something. She sat up. 'Clem said she's got one more thing to tell us, Ludo.'

58

Back in the cinema pod, the screen crackled and flickered while reception was established with New York.

Clem was in the middle of a fitting. She shooed her **V.I.P.** off camera, before
MEANING: Very Important Person
Coco could see who it was.

Clem turned to her daughter.

'Someone else is coming to Sydney very soon, darling, to make up for me not being there. And they have a (personal message) just for you. Take it away, boss.'

STEP
FORWARD...
Who is it?
Can Coco cope with any more surprises today?

'Hey,' Prince Louis giggled to the camera. 'Coco, yeah?'

Coco was as still as a statue. As if she had just been **electrocuted.** She nodded, speechless.

'Yeah, so I've got this top secret **gig** coming up in Sydney,' Louis said. 'It's, like, really small. I'm testing out some new songs and need some **sunshine** real bad. It's just going to be industry dudes. But your **M.U.M.** – hey, the best stylist in the world – has two **front-row** tickets here. For you. And, ah . . . **M.** Yeah.'

M.? Who's M.?

A **whisper** came from off-camera. '*N. N.*'

'Oh yeah.' **Louis** laughed. 'N. That little mate of yours with the pirate scarf. I saw you both on your mum's phone. So hey, Coco, I'll see you in the sunshine. Check ya later!'

Coco flopped backwards onto the velvet cushions. And stayed there. In **shock.**

A while back, she and N had been given **backstage passes** to a Prince Louis concert, but he'd cancelled the tour when he **broke** his leg and arm in five places in a snowboarding accident. Coco **never ever** thought she'd get a golden Louis ticket **again.**

The most amazing surprise EVER.

COCO woke bright and early the next morning. It was time to crank the ○ super pop-tacular SIGNAL MACHINE into action.

It had **25** signals that it could shoot from Coco's chimney, depending on the message. At 8 o'clock on the dot, **N** would be at her bedroom window, with binoculars, ready for the **BANJO FANDANGO DAILY SIGNAL!**

N knew the signals off by heart. (She was the class swot, after all.)

The Signal Machine is especially pretty with coloured paper planes.

But there was **one** signal Coco had never programmed the machine to do before . . .

The **Signal** of **Spectacular** Signals: a spray of shiny silver and red and gold and black confetti, like a beautiful volcano.

Now this'll be interesting.

N had to look up the Handbook of Interpretation to find out what the confetti meant.

The message was:

Meet at CADI BEACH in half an hour because there is:

The most URGENT INCREDIBLE UNBELIEVABLE news EVER.
And I I have to tell you or I'll BURST.

So glad we got to finally see this signal. We've been waiting.

The girls met at Cadi Beach.  N listened to Coco's news about the **Prince Louis** concert with her mouth open in shock, then she flopped backwards onto the sand. And stayed there. Still in shock.

Prince
Louis's
Number 2
biggest fan
(after Coco)

N was only brought back to reality by Coco's news that Prince Louis had complimented N's pirate scarf after seeing it on Clem's phone.

Wowsers.
N is a fashion
icon.

Urgent Question of the Day: **What** would the girls wear to the concert?

They looked at each other, blank.

'No fashion challenge has ever defeated us,' Coco declared.

Coco turned and pointed towards the south.

'To **Hot Bright** we must go,' she said.

squealed in excitement. Hot Bright was a favourite shop of theirs.

It was full of bolts of tiger–striped velvet and fluoro tulle and lace ribbons and golden rope and giant pompoms and pipe cleaners and parachute silk.

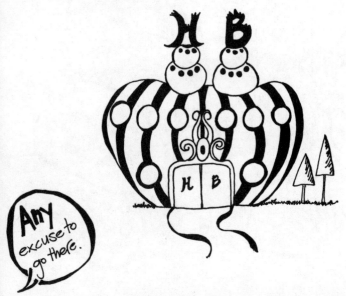

Any excuse to go there.

The girls jumped on the **745** bus. They spied **Miss Bonkiss** and Mr Patilla up the back.

Gasp!

Sitting **really** close together.

Double **gasp!**

With eyes only for each other.

Triple **gasp!**

The girls sat as far away as **possible** from the disturbing sight.

Giggle giggle.

Apple Button got on the bus with her mum.

Coco and N told her **not** to look up the back. Apple couldn't help it.

Banksia Bay Public cannot cope with this teacherly development.

When Coco and N told Apple about their **Prince Louis** tickets, she flopped backwards onto the bus seat. And stayed there. In shock.

Her mum looked at her in **horror**.

Apple? Is this about a BOY?

You're **allergic** to strobe lighting.

They have strobe lighting at concerts like that.

Boys, no, please don't tell me that's started already.

'This is not just any boy, Mrs Button,' Coco said. 'It's ~~the~~ boy.'

Keep up, Mrs B. You've a lot to learn about your daughter's world.

Apple sat bolt upright, and asked Coco the question she was **dreading.**

Coco had already asked Clem if she could get more tickets, but the answer was . It was a very special, very small concert – and Coco and N had been squeezed in.

Coco shook her head. She felt

'Doesn't matter.' **Apple** smiled, being very **brave**. 'I'll just lie on my bed on the night, listening to all my favourite **Louis** songs. *Not* in the dark,' she added.

Coco and N *giggled*. Apple was known for being terrified of the dark.

As demonstrated in *Coco Banjo Has Been Unfriended*

'**Hey**,' Coco declared, 'why don't we have a Cha Cha sleepover the night after the concert – with the lights on *all night*?'

Coco Banjo: heart-lifter.

Apple waved goodbye to her friends when the bus got to the shops.

Coco and N could barely contain their excitement. They ran into *Hot Bright*:

M   Straight to the feather boa section

M   Then to red Chinese silk for wedding dresses

M   Then to giant foam balls

M   Then to sequins and spangles.

WHAT to wear?

Too much choice here, girls.

The two girls ended up in a **heap** on the floor, covered in scraps of velvet and satin and crazy hats and giant pompoms and clouds of parachute silk.

So covered, in fact, that they could not see out.

'Well, well, well,'

said a voice above them. 'I'd know those shoes anywhere – ewwwww.'

The voice sounded **disgusted.**
It was a voice the girls had been hoping not to hear all summer holidays. And it belonged to **ONE** person, and **ONE** person only . . .

It was **Belle Pratt-Perkins.**

Coco scrambled away from the parachute silk, her heart sinking. 'Hi, Belle.'

'Great outfit, Coco,' their classmate **sneered** as she looked at the mess. 'Is that your latest ... creation?'

Why did Belle have to be here?

Belle has the Trample-like ability to make Coco feel about a centimetre tall.

jumped up. 'We're going to a top secret Prince Louis concert,' she exclaimed proudly. 'And we're working out what to wear.'

P-p-prince Louis?' Belle stumbled. Blushed. Couldn't believe what she was hearing. 'Did you say . . .?'

Coco nodded. Smiled. Enjoyed her moment of triumph.

They all knew that Belle was Prince Louis's Number 3 Fan in the world.

Right after Coco and N.

Belle extended a hand, strongly, to . Then **Coco**. Hauled them out of the mess they were in.

'Always my pleasure,' she *purred*.

'That's **not** going to get you a ticket, Belle,' N said.

'My mum could only get **2**,' Coco explained apologetically.

Belle looked at them both. Went redder and redder. **Screwed** up her face.

Goodness, is she going to explode?

82

Belle's mother *rushed* over from another aisle.

Mrs Pratt–Perkins glared at Coco and N when she saw them. '**What** have you done to my baby girl?'

Tearfully, Belle explained the situation.

Mrs Pratt–Perkins stepped back. Curled in her lips, thinking really hard. Stared at COCO and .

Oh really?

'One thousand dollars,' Mrs Pratt-Perkins said.

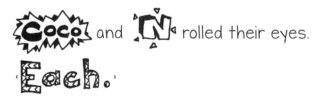 and rolled their eyes.

'Each.'

Coco and N double-rolled their eyes.

No can do. These golden tickets are NOT for sale.

Belle walked right in front of her mother and put her hands on her hips.

'Mummy, if you don't get me a ticket then I'll vomit all over Miss Trample's meal when she comes over for Christmas lunch. I will. I really, really will.'

Coco and **N** were open-mouthed. Miss Trample was going to the *Pratt-Perkins'* house for Christmas lunch?

Hope they've got lots of toilet paper.

So ***that's*** how Belle got all those awards and assembly mentions and leadership roles and photos in the school magazine. (Only beaten in that department by pictures of one "Miss" Gladys Trample.)

PHOTO NUMBER 248 of the year.

It's a very *cosy* arrangement.

As **Belle** went redder and redder, her mother went more purple.

Mrs Pratt–Perkins came right up close to Coco. 'We'll give you a **shoutout** on Belle's Instagram account. As of this morning she has **105,000** followers. Across the globe.'

Internet superstar

Models designer clothes that she gets for free

Quite a little business she's got going there

Miss Pratt–Perkins looked Coco up and down. Couldn't help a **sneer**, just like her daughter.

'We'll even give a push to your little . . . creations,' she said.

Oh, she's a piece of work.

Coco looked down at her outfit. Attempted to wipe the **fluff** off it. Looked up, at Belle's mother, straight in the eye.

'I'm **SO** sorry I can't help you, Mrs Pratt-Perkins. I would if I could. But the tickets are as scarce as hen's teeth and my mum could only get two.'

And with that, Coco and N walked away. With as much *dignity* as they could muster while having bits of velvet ribbon, lace, feathers and sequins stuck all over them.

That'll show her.

'I'll get them on **ebaY**!' Belle's mother screeched to the girls' departing backs. 'And did you say your *mother*? I don't think she really exists, Coco Banjo. No one does. She's a **figment** of your imagination, isn't she?'

Like mother, like daughter.

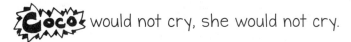 would not cry, she would not cry.

But those flung words **hurt**.

Grown-ups weren't meant to be so . . . so . . . *childish.*

And how *awful* if they ended up sitting next to Belle at the secret concert.

Belle *always* gets her way.

She's *very* used to winning.

She has a *lot of help* with it.

'Let's go back to the **sequin** section, N,' Coco declared, refusing to let this Belle—shaped setback get her down. 'I've got an idea.'

'Way to go, girl!' gave **COCO** a huge squeezy cuddle of awesomeness. 'Just get that creating cap on, so we can wipe the past five minutes from our minds.'

and upwards!

Coco was ready to create. But she needed inspiration.

This called for the **Creation Pod**.

Coco's all-time favourite room

The room was crammed with painter's easels and a potter's wheel and a sewing machine, a tool bench and craft boxes, art cupboards and a Lego table. Basically, it was full of **everything** Coco might need for making stuff.

Ludo adored it too. So much to yelp at! So many ribbons to get entangled in! So many balls of wool to play soccer with!

The room that swallows time.

It was **BLISS.**

Coco wheeled the Skip Back Machine into the room and pedalled it into glorious motion. **Glems** memories played to inspire her.

Then Coco started creating outfits. For  and her. For their upcoming night of deliciousness.

Coco has never worked on a project so exciting.

She stayed up **all night** in a feverish fever of creating.

Who needed sleep when there were far more important, Louis-related tasks to be completed?

In the early hours of the morning, she **finally** glanced up at the clock.

Dawn! The kookaburras and cockatoos and rosellas were just getting up!

Coco finally stumbled to bed.

About time, dear girl!

97

Coco woke at **midday.**

That's what summer holidays were for . . .

(**Miss Bonkiss** says all [BANKSIA BAY PUBLIC] kids need **huge** sleep-ins on the holidays. And at least one day of staying in their jarmies all day.)

Coco decided that *this* would be her 'All-Day Amazing PJ Day'.

Coco had **missed** the 8 o'clock Signal Machine appointment with N. She *raced* outside anyway, binoculars  around her neck.

She looked across the water to N's bedroom.

Then *froze*.

What's happened? Quick, tell us!

's bedroom window had a towel across it. It was black. With white stars. It was . . .

THE TOWEL

of

DOOM

MEANING: All was not well in N–Land. All was horribly terrible, in fact. The only other time N had hung it up was when her mother made her miss **Apple's** ice-skating party at Bondi Beach because N hadn't done enough practice for her violin exam.

Mrs N can be scary. Especially when exams are involved.

 cranked up the Signal Machine.

Out of her chimney burst a spray of stale
Weet-Bix. This meant:

I'm here for you, sister. I'll be at **Cadi Beach** in twenty minutes. See you THERE.

The Towel of Doom means 100 per cent *bad*.

When  rowboat arrived at Cadi Beach, N. was already there.

'My parents won't let me go to the concert!' N cried across to Coco.

It couldn't be true! Especially after Coco had spent the night making the *perfect* N–meets–Louis outfit!

. was sobbing as she rushed forward to help  drag her rowboat up the sand.

'My mum said I wasn't even allowed to see you today because I had to have a "**slow**" day,' N cried.

The girls looked at each other.   They knew what that meant.

'Something just **snapped** in me.' N's face
looked wild, as if she was being hunted.
'I knew that you'd be spending the night
making our outfits. I wanted to see them.
Desperately. Today. I **had** to.'

She gulped.

'My parents told me to go to my room,'
N continued. 'I wasn't thinking right. I went
Louis-crazy. Just crazy. I got my violin. Threw
it out my window so hard it cracked on the
pebbles around the swimming pool. Then
bounced. And . . . *fell* in.'

Coco gasped. **N** had never been like this,
ever. She was, after all:

The GOODEST good girl in the SCHOOL.

Wow. We are stunned.

N. threw herself on the sand. Wailed that her parents had completely **banned** her from going to the concert.

In fact, the day before the concert, the whole family would now be packing up their caravan and heading up the coast for a **camping** trip.

'To that boring mangrove swamp at that boring lake we always go to. And you know how **allergic** I am to mosquitoes,' N cried.

Coco looked at her friend. **N** was broken. Completely. Coco had never seen her like this. The **Prince Louis** concert was going to be the **best** night of N's life. And now she wasn't going.

It was unimaginable. Unbearable. Beyond pain.

As Coco would be dancing and singing right in front of Louis — so **close** she could almost touch him — N would be stuck in a sagging tent. Trying to swat a whining mozzie. That she couldn't see.

AGONY.

Coco bit her lip. She couldn't **bear** this. They were best mates, after all. N's pain was hers.

There was only **one** thing she could do . . .

'I'm not going to the concert either,' she said quietly. 'I can't go without you, N. It wouldn't be *right*.'

'No, no, no!'

N said.

Love you, N girl.

Even more than Louis.

But Coco was firm. 'Best mates have to be **loyal**. It's what I want to do.'

You are one very special friend, Coco Banjo.

What followed was the  biggest cuddle of awesomeness that had ever happened.

Then . looked over to her house and said she'd better be getting home before her parents realised she had snuck out her window and climbed down the drainpipe.

Naughtiness piling on naughtiness here.

'Now we just need to work out who gets those tickets,' Coco said.

They looked at each other.

Well there is someone who's mighty keen.

Who?

It hurt, really hurt, to give away the most
precious tickets in the world – but Coco had
to do it. It wasn't fair on N.

She asked Apple Button if she wanted them:

'Well then, why don't you come for a sleepover
at my place on the night of the concert
instead?' Coco suggested.

Coco asked *Jay Page* if he wanted the tickets:

Coco thought of giving the tickets to **Miss Bonkiss**, but she suspected Miss Bonkiss only had eyes for one boy right now . . .

Coco even thought she should give the tickets to her guardian, aging rock star **Rick Ragger...**

But she decided Rick might be too traumatised by what the younger generation were doing on stage now.

That night, in the cinema pod, Coco asked **Clem, what** to do.

'I am soooooo proud of you, Missy Princess Pie, for making this decision. What a *great* friend you are,' her mum said. Then Clem had a think.

There's just been a terrible earthquake in Tibet

Why don't you raise some money for charity

A lemonade Stall

With chocolate brownies

Doing something for charity is always an excellent idea.

 Coco

exclaimed. She was on her mum's wavelength. 'And then two of the brownies, inside, can have **secret** coins. And the people who get those coins get the tickets!'

Perfect! Clem said.

Coco waited several days for Mrs N to calm down. *She always does*

Then Coco invited **N**, Apple, **Jay**, and Jay's best mate, **Harry**, for a Mass Cooking Extravaganza.

The Fabulous Five assembled on **CHA CHA ISLAND**. Then they went bonkers with all the amazing gadgets in the kitchen pod.

Best kitchen ever.

Best fun ever.

Coco needed *special* coins. She remembered she had two old pennies from 1966. They could be the magic tokens to be cooked into the brownies.

The five kids made the most enormous, delicious, bowl–licky **mess**.

Is there, er, any brownie mixture left in the bowl?

The Fabulous Five then invaded the
Creation Pod.

They made posters to stick to power poles
around the neighbourhood.

Can these kids get any muckier?

121

Word spread like **Wildfire** throughout the

neighbourhood.

Excitement built.

Who would win the coins?

It's going to be a **very** big Sunday.

Sunday morning arrived. It was a **gorgeous**, **sparkly** Sydney day.

The Fabulous Five headed across from **CHA CHA ISLAND** with their precious cargo. **Coco** and **N** were in their rowboats. **Jay** was on his stand-up paddle board. **Apple** was in her kayak. **Harry** was on his Laser sailboat.

No, Jay is **not** being entrusted with any brownies.

Mrs N had set up a picnic table for the stall.

She may be feeling guilty here.

There was already an 𝙴𝙽𝙾𝚁𝙼𝙾𝚄𝚂

queue.

←WOW

Word has spread far and wide.

The Fabulous Five didn't know if they had enough brownies for the people who were already here – let alone anyone else who came! What would they do?

They looked at each other.

'Leave it to me,' Coco said.

She stood on a chair and announced:

Due to popular demand there will only be ONE brownie sold per person. Repeat, one.

Good thinking, Coco.

They started to sell brownies and lemonade to the people at the **Front** of the queue.

Everyone ripped open the slabs of chocolate yumminess with their hands or their teeth, **desperate** for the coin that would win them the tickets.

But someone was pushing their way through the crowd.

Belle.

Of course.

Just featured on Instagram

Along with waterploof phone holder and mirrored swimming goggles.

Belle stalked straight up to **Coco**, with her parents close behind her.

'I want 200 dollars worth of brownies. **IMMEDIATELY!** Belle said.

How many brownies was Belle planning on eating here?

The brownies were 2 dollars each. Coco did the maths.

Just for **Belle**!

'Rules are rules,' Coco said firmly. '**ONE** brownie per person.'

'And you have to get back in line,' added.

'No pushing in,' *Jay* said.

Would Belle and her parents do as they were asked?

'You know, Belle, you could always donate your extra brownie money to a *good* cause,' Coco said with a smile. 'After all, you have 200 dollars there.'

'I need to save for my **pedicures**,' Belle screamed. 'And blow–dries. And why are there so many people here? **URGH.**'

Then she and her parents stomped back to the end of the queue.

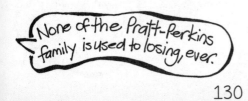

None of the Pratt-Perkins family is used to losing, ever.

One by one the locals of Banksia Bay bought their brownies and scurried away, *ripping* them open to see if the lucky coin would be theirs.

From all over the car park came anguished cries.

The piles of brownies quickly went down. The piles of money for Tibet quickly rose.

There was still **NO SIGN** of the precious pennies.

Did they fall out in the cooking process?

Finally . . . it was **Belle's** turn.

Strangely, Belle's group seemed to have
grown while she was waiting in the
queue.

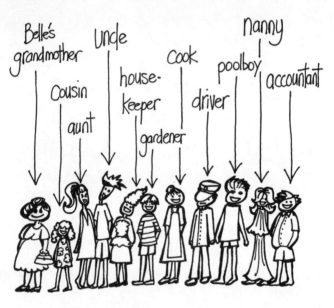

A hush fell over the crowd. The Pratt–Perkins
family **ALWAYS** got their way. Would it
happen again?

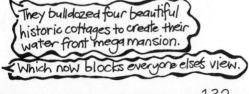

They bulldozed four beautiful
historic cottages to create their
water front mega mansion.

Which now blocks everyone else's view.

Belle bought a brownie. No luck.

Her father bought one. Her mother bought one. No luck, no luck. Her grandmother. No luck.

One by one the Pratt-Perkins' staff bought their brownies.

It got to the last Belle-helper. The nanny.

N. was trembling as she took the nanny's money. **Harry** was trembling as he handed over a brownie.

The nanny took a bite and . . .

The suspense is killing us!

. . . said,

Because she'd bitten down on something hard.

 looked at **Belle**. Right. So she now got to go to the bestest best concert in the entire world. Yep, Belle had **WON** again.

That's the way the brownie crumbles.

Belle ran triumphantly around the car park with her arms in the air. 'Yes! Yes! Yes!' she shouted.

Coco suddenly wished her mum was here. Achingly.

Clem was never, ever here when she was needed.

This hurts.

But hang on, who would get the other coin?

The crowd was thinning now that **Belle** was a winner. (No one wanted to have to sit next to Belle and listen to her **Shrieking** all night.)

Come on, everyone, keep buying!

The people of Tibet need more donations!

There were only a few brownies left at the lemonade stall.  **Coco** was busy counting the huge amount of money the Fabulous Five had raised for Tibet. *Hooray!*

Suddenly, more people arrived in the queue. Coco looked up.

The late arrivals were Kourtney, Tiffany, and Saffron, who was Belle's new neighbour. All of **Belle's** best friends. And of course she wanted one of her mates to get the other ticket.

All mini Belles wearing Belle's designer cast-offs.

Kourtney, Tiffany and Saffron eagerly bought their brownies and tore them open with their teeth.

There were only a few brownies left. Would **anyone** buy the brownie with the second ticket?

A familiar loud voice rang out through the car park.

And then the owner of the loud voice appeared. In full hiking glory, ready to traverse the mighty headlands of Sydney . . .

Miss Trample.

Loving that hiking stick, Miss Trample.

Miss Trample's hiking companion, Beryl, stepped forward first.

'I've got a *good* feeling about this, Gladys,' she said. 'I go all fluttery at the thought of royalty. This is my lucky day!'

But yet again with these cheeky brownies . . .

Then Miss Trample paid her  dollars.

'Just what I need to give me energy for a hearty 𝕗𝕚𝕧𝕖 –kilometre walk, Beryl!' she said.

She took a 𝓱𝓾𝓰𝓮 bite. The whole car park was, once again, completely silent. Watching in awe.

Chew faster, Miss Trample.

Miss Trample stopped.

Pulled an **awful** face.

Pulled out of her crumb-infested mouth . . .
a .

All the kids in the car park stepped forward, overcome by the huge **awfulness** of the situation.

A ticket to **Prince Louis** – completely wasted!

Miss Trample didn't even know **who** he was!

Jay cried: 'Miss Trample, it's really loud music. A pop concert. Your ears will **burst**.'

Apple whispered: 'There's **strobe** lighting. You'll go crazy.'

Harry said: 'You'll get squashed in the mosh pit because you're right up the **front**.'

N added: 'You'll be pushed up against all the other kids around you and they'll be really **sweaty** and **stinky**.'

The horror, the horror!

How will Miss Trample cope?

Coco stepped forward. 'Miss Trample, it will be worse than when I do my drumming lesson right above your **office**.'

Miss Trample looked around at everyone, horrified.

She turned to **Belle**, who was looking equally horrified.

Belle could not move or speak. She was completely frozen. In **SHOCK**.

Oh dear. Explosion coming.

This was not good. **Coco** had to turn this situation around. She stepped out in front of the table.

She announced to the crowd that the lemonade, brownies and private donations had raised – amazingly – over **1,000** dollars for the Tibetan earthquake appeal.

Coco smiled. 'Pat yourselves on the back, guys. Really **well done**.'

Result!

Coco took **Belle's** hand, then Miss Trample's. She raised their arms **high**.

Took a deep breath. Didn't show anyone how much it **hurt** to say this:

'And these are the winners of the two very precious Prince Louis tickets. **Congratolations** !'

There was an awkward pause . . .

How can Belle turn **this** into a winning situation?

Coco jumped in again. 'Unless, that is, you two winners would like to donate the prizes to someone in the crowd who's more . . . ah . . . er . . .' (She wanted to say *deserving* but couldn't.)

Belle's face turned purple. Like, yes, she was going to ⚡*explode*⚡ This happened a lot when she didn't get her way.

I really, really want to go. Just **not** with...

The crowd is gasping.

Miss Trample spoke over the top of her.

'I'd **love** to go, thank you very much. I need to learn more about my students. Need to understand what makes the young nowadays tick.'

a shudder

Watch out, kids.

Mr Pratt–Perkins stepped forward.

'Well, that settles it then. Belle and Miss Trample will be seeing the **top secret** concert with this Prince . . .'

He had a *think*, but was struggling. 'L–L–Liam?'

Every child in the crowd cried the answer.

Yep, there were a lot of sad kids that day.

Coco packed up the lemonade stand with a heavy heart. She, like **Apple**, would now be singing **Louis** songs on her bed during his concert.

She waved goodbye to her friends then rowed back home to **CHA CHA ISLAND**.

Ludo is going to get a **LOT** of big, teary cuddles when they get home.

That night, Coco lay on Clem's super-wide bed and played her Skip Back Machine over and over and over.

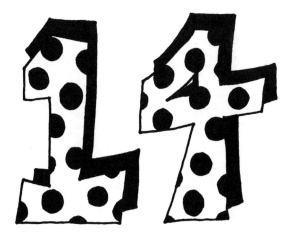

It was the night of the **Prince Louis** concert.

It was pouring **rain**. In fact, it had been solidly raining for two entire days. A typically Sydney, thunderous, tropical summer downpour.

This had meant:

⋙ No swimming with Daisy

⋙ No playing with **Wing** and **Wang** on the beach

⋙ No taking *Ludo* for long walks.

This summer holiday was NOT turning out to be Coco's idea of a super wow one, in any way.

But on the plus side, it also meant 's family did not go **camping** after all.

Mr N is secretly relieved too.

He HATES camping. Especially setting up tents.

Mrs N was feeling guilty about the **harshness** of her daughter's enormous, no-concert punishment.

Worst ever

She couldn't get the tickets back, but to make up for it she let have a sleepover at **Cocos** that night.

N's big sister, **Natarsha**, was babysitting them.

Now this will be **fun.**

$\bigstar$Natarsha was a great **disappointment** to her parents, because she:

- 🎴 Was not in the streamed class at high school

- 🎴 Only got up to Grade Two in violin

- 🎴 Had coloured her hair

- 🎴 Had declared that she wanted to be a music producer instead of becoming a dentist like her dad.

Coco thought Natarsha was *fabulous* – and told her so, often.

Coco is a heart-lifter.

Apple Button was also staying for a sleepover.

Coco had promised to leave on a night-light for the entire sleep.

She had made Apple a special Louis outfit. To go with the ones she had made for N and herself. For the concert that they were not going to.

The girls could hear the **thump** of Louis's music from across the harbour. They imagined **Belle** and Miss Trample dancing away at the very front.

Unbearable.

This is not good.

They tried singing along but they couldn't make out the songs. And they couldn't sing **Louis** tunes without getting all **teary**.

Coco, do something, fast.

'Let's make up our **OWN** songs!' Coco yelled.

And so with Natarsha's help, they did. To drown out the thump of the concert.

BAND NOW KNOWN AS **EN-CEE-AY**

N C A

Together **Coco**, **N** and **Apple** created **3** fabulous songs:

'*Reason*'

'*Fire*' and

'*Direction*'.

Keep it up and you'll go far, girlies!

The girls stayed up deliciously late:

- Having **midnight** feasts (at 8 pm, 8.30 pm, 9 pm and 9.30 pm)

- Changing their outfits  times

- Painting their **nails**

- Spray-painting their hair then putting **glitter** in it

- Spray-painting the top bit of *Ludo's* fur then putting glitter in it.

Matching!

Natarsha let them do whatever they want.
She was the **B.B.E.**

what?

She's definitely going to be invited back.

The girls ended up having a *bath*.

Then they flopped into their  sheepskin-covered, blow-up sleepover beds. In their matching animal onesies. Exhausted.

Snuggle heaven

Onesie envy here.

 and **Apple** quickly fell asleep.

So did **Natarsha** in the next room.

Too many late nights on Garage Band, madam.

But  was wide awake.

Belle would probably be at **Louis's** stage door by now, at the front of the crowd, waiting for her selfie with him.

She would post it instantly. **Double** her Instagram followers overnight, knowing her.

Belle sure knows how to make things happen for herself.

COCO and *Ludo* went down to the beach and sat side by side on the sand.

They looked across the water to **Prince Louis's** concert. There was no more distant thump of music. It was over. The band must be packing up. Everyone must be getting ready to go home.

Coco cuddled Ludo tight. The puppy sensed something was wrong with his big sister, and licked her face with adorable little *kisses*.

Best. Pet. Ever.

Suddenly, Coco heard a **noise**.

The **blaring** of a ship horn.

Really **close** to **CHA CHA ISLAND**

Eh? What on **earth** could it be?

It sounded again. **Closer**.

Coco ran to wake up **N**, **Apple** and **Natarsha** and they **dashed** outside. All in their onesies.

What a **sight** you are, girls.

The girls stood in a line along Cha Cha Beach. With *Ludo*, and **Wing and Wang**, who'd all been woken from their slumbers by the huge commotion.

Directly in front of **CHA CHA ISLAND** was now a **super-sleek** superyacht. Anchored. All its lights blaring.

In front of the superyacht was a small speedboat, rapidly making its way towards them.

It was too **dark** for the girls to see who was in it.

WHAT is going on here?

A shadowy figure stepped from the speedboat onto Cha Cha Island's little wooden jetty.

It **was** ... it **was** ...
it **was** ...

Come on,
spill the
beans.

Prince Louis!!!!!!

'Well, that was my secret concert,' he grinned, walking towards the girls. 'With several hundred people. But now it's time for my secret secret, very private, very exclusive, best concert **EVER**.'

Whaaaaaat?

All four girls flopped backwards onto the sand. And stayed there. In giggly **shock**.

All the girls *leapt* up and raced towards their pop idol.

'I've only got one hour, so let's get this show on the road!' **Louis** said.

Everyone squealed and screamed with **excitement**. But from behind Prince Louis, **Coco** heard a sound.

She left the excited huddle.

Because **someone else** was climbing onto the jetty. Someone they hadn't noticed in all the excitement. Someone who was **singing**, ever so softly . . .

It was **CLEM.**

Standing there, in really real life, waiting for her daughter to notice. With **tears** in her eyes.

Singing, 'Tick tock tick tock, it's Clem on the dot on the cuddle–time clock.'

Coco raced into her mum's arms. 'You surprised me! You surprised me!'

'Oh, I'm rather **good** at surprises,' Clem laughed, squeezing Coco tight.

Sorry, Louis, but **this** is actually the best surprise ever.

Cuddle of Awesomeness

As they *joyously* walked towards the others, Clem asked Coco if that headmistress had been mean to Coco lately.

Coco thought back to what Miss Trample had said at the **supermarket**. 'Ooooh yes,' she said.

'Well then,' **Clem** said, 'I'm hanging around here until school starts again, Missy Princess Pie. I'll do the tuckshop and the clothing pool and be the zebra–crossing lollipop lady and help out with the cooking classes. I'll volunteer for **everything**. I'll show that Miss, er, whatsername . . . Vample?'

'Trample, Mum, Miss Trample.'

Banksia Bay Public won't know what's hit it.

Coco thought of **Clem's**:

- Non-existent *cooking* skills

- **Traffic** marshalling qualities

- **Appalled** face whenever Clem caught sight of the drab school uniform (which the clothing pool was full of)

- **Glamorous** outfits.

Clem will start a new fashion trend here, no doubt.

'Are you sure about this, Mum?' **COCO** said.

CLEM'S eyes were shining. 'Girlfriend, we are on.'

They **high-fived** so hugely they almost knocked each other over.

We think Miss Coco needs a high-vis vest too.

What followed was Coco Banjo's best,
super WOW summer holiday EVER.

Because it had:

- ▨ Sunshine every day

- ▨ Lots of swimming

- ▨ Lots of playing with  (and *Wing* and *Wang*, and *DAISY*)

- ▨ Lots of visits to the supermarket for all her new school stationery ✏️

Wooohoooo!

Coco loves stationery.

- And, most of all, lots and lots of *MUM*
- With the best *pet* ever, always trying to snuggle in between them.

N.J. GEMMELL

according to the people who know her the most
(her four kids)

She can't cook. She sometimes feeds us porridge for dinner (with banana on top). She hides behind the kitchen cupboard door and eats all the chocolate biscuits when she thinks we're not looking. She is often the World's Most Embarrassing Mum. She gets really happy when she's writing (it stops her being Shouty Mum). She has written another series for kids called The Kensington Reptilarium, The Icicle Illuminarium and The Luna Laboratorium. It's about four Aussie bush kids who are even grubbier and cheekier than us. (N.J. Gemmell says this is not possible) She dreams of one day passing on the title of World's Most Embarrassing Mum to someone else.